SAMMY'S STORY

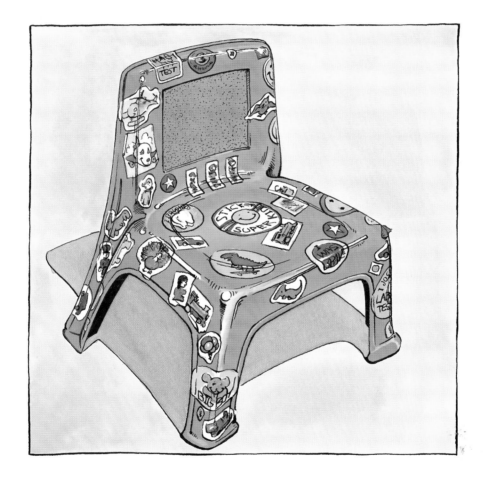

DAVID KOOHARIAN

A DK INK BOOK

DK PUBLISHING, INC.
NEW YORK

WHILE SAMMY SLEPT, THE SNOW STOPPED AND THE SKY CLEARED. THAT'S WHEN THREE FUNNY GUYS BEGAN TO SEARCH FOR HIM.

FOR SEVERAL HOURS THEY RAN THROUGH THE NEIGHBORHOOD LOOKING IN WINDOWS AND WAKING UP DOGS. FINALLY, THEY FOUND THE RIGHT HOUSE AND EVENTUALLY THE RIGHT WINDOW.

THE WINDOW WAS LOCKED AS ONE MIGHT EXPECT BUT THESE WERE CLEVER GUYS AND IN NO TIME AT ALL THEY WERE CLIMBING INSIDE.

"BUT I CAN'T GO...I CAN'T WALK."

"CAN'T WALK? THAT'S TERRIBLE. WHY CAN'T YOU WALK?"

"I DON'T KNOW... NO ONE KNOWS. I JUST GET WEAKER AND WEAKER INSTEAD OF STRONGER."

"I'M SORRY. THAT SOUNDS SCARY. ARE YOU SCARED?"

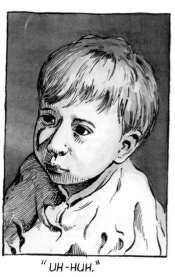

"UH-HUH."

"WELL, IF WE CAN THINK OF SOMETHING, WOULD YOU COME WITH US?"

"UH-HUH."

SAMMY'S FATHER HAD BUILT HIM A SPECIAL SLED AND IT WAS JUST THE THING THE GUYS NEEDED. ORVILLE, LENNY, AND REGINALD GRABBED THE ROPE AND OFF THEY WENT AS FAST AS THEY COULD RUN.

AT THE END OF THE STREET, THEY DISAPPEARED INTO THE TREES.

ON AND ON THEY RAN WITH SAMMY IN TOW, DEEPER AND DEEPER INTO THE WOODS...

WHEN THEY CAME OUT OF THE WOODS, THEY WERE NO LONGER IN SAMMY'S TOWN OR ANYWHERE HE HAD EVER BEEN. THEY CLIMBED HIGH INTO THE MOUNTAINS. FAR AHEAD SAMMY COULD SEE THE GLOW OF A SMALL FIRE.

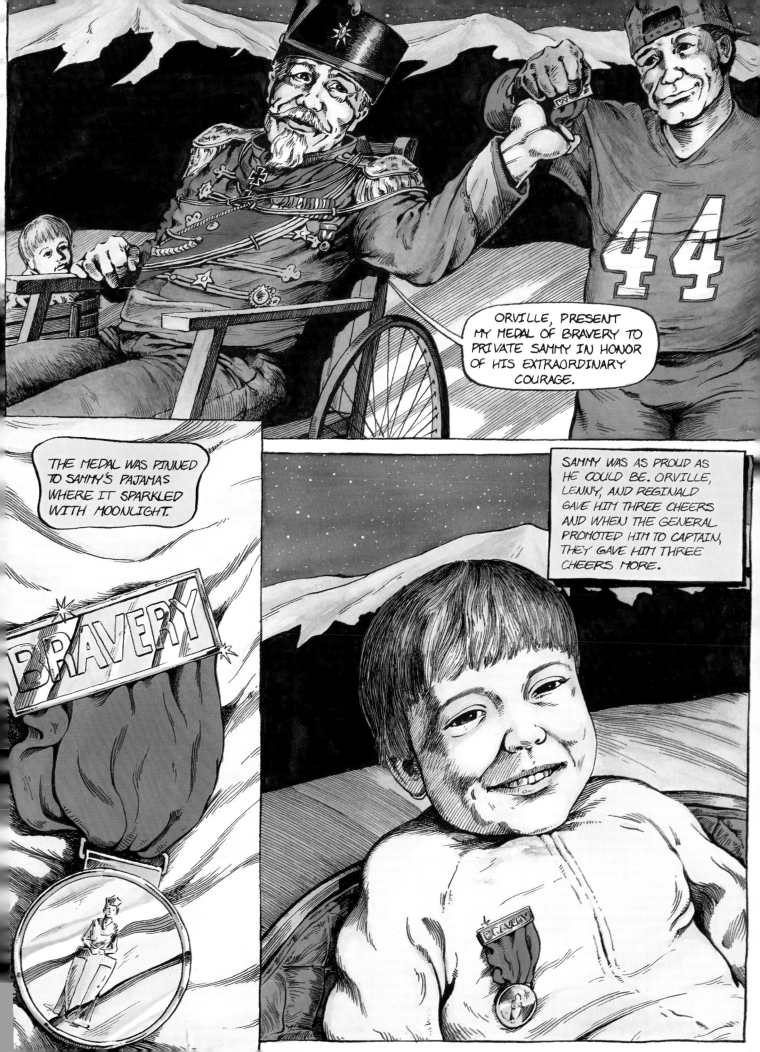

THROUGH THE FROZEN NIGHT AIR THEY RACED TOWARDS THE ZARGON'S MOUNTAIN. THE FARTHER THEY WENT THE STRONGER FENRIS BECAME. HE LOVED TO RUN AND PULL.

BEFORE LONG SAMMY SAW THE RED GLOW OF THE ZARGON'S CAVE. AN INSTANT LATER THEY DISAPPEARED INTO THE ENTRANCE.

FENRIS PULLED THE SLED AS CLOSE TO THE ZARGON'S CHAIR AS POSSIBLE. FROM THERE SAMMY HAD TO CLIMB OUT OF HIS SLED AND CRAWL TO THE BOTTOM STEP.

SAMMY FELT VERY WEAK AND UNSTEADY. HIS CRAWLING WAS SLOW BUT HE WAS DETERMINED, AND AT LAST HE REACHED THE FOOT OF THE ZARGON'S CHAIR.

SAMMY LOOKED UP AND SAW DEWDROP SITTING THERE, ALL FURRY. SAMMY COULD SEE WHY THE GENERAL MISSED HIM SO MUCH. THE ZARGON'S CHAIR WAS VERY HIGH. SAMMY KNEW THERE WAS NO WAY HE COULD REACH DEWDROP UNLESS HE STOOD UP. HIS HEART SANK. SAMMY HADN'T HAD THE STRENGTH TO STAND UP IN A LONG TIME.

SAMMY DIDN'T KNOW IF HE COULD STAND OR NOT BUT HE KNEW HE HAD TO TRY. HE WOULD NOT GIVE UP. HE HELD ON TO THE CHAIR AND WITH GREAT EFFORT HE PULLED HIMSELF UP. HIS FRAGILE BODY WAS SHAKING AS HE CLUNG TIGHTLY TO THE CHAIR WITH BOTH HANDS.

DEWDROP WAS NOW WITHIN REACH. IF ONLY HE COULD GRAB HIM BEFORE HE FELL DOWN.

HE STEADIED HIMSELF AS BEST HE COULD AND REACHED UP AND GRASPED DEWDROP.

THE INSTANT SAMMY GRASPED DEWDROP, THE ZARGON APPEARED.

STOP! WHO DARES TO LAY A HAND ON MY DEWDROP? I'LL HAVE MY VENGEANCE. YOU CAN'T ESCAPE ME!

SAMMY CLUTCHED DEWDROP AND FELL TO HIS KNEES. HE REACHED FOR HIS MEDAL. A SUDDEN SENSE OF TERROR AND DOOM SWEPT OVER HIM... THE MEDAL WAS GONE!

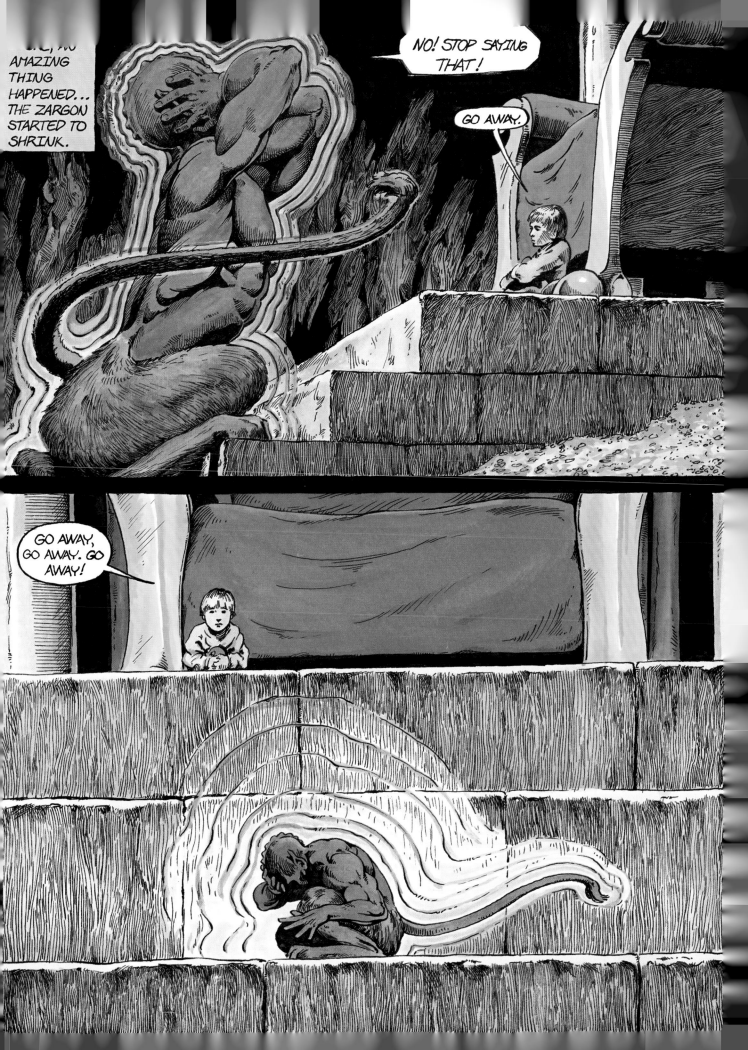

THE HALL WAS EMPTY. SAMMY CALLED FOR FENRIS BUT COULDN'T FIND HIM. THE ZARGON HAD FRIGHTENED HIM AWAY.

SAMMY SAT ALONE FOR AWHILE AND THEN BEGAN TO CRAWL OUT, THROWING DEWDROP AHEAD OF HIM AND CALLING FOR FENRIS AS HE WENT.

AFTER A LONG TIME SAMMY FINALLY CRAWLED OUT OF THE CAVE AND AWAY FROM THE MOUNTAIN. THEN HE NOTICED THAT IT HAD BECOME WARM, ALMOST HOT OUTSIDE. THE SNOW HAD MELTED AND IN THE EAST THE SUN WAS RISING. SAMMY SAT, RESTING WITH DEWDROP, AND WATCHED THE DAWN.

ED MOVED HIS HAND AND SAMMY SAW ONLY DARKNESS. OUT OF THE DARKNESS CAME BRILLIANT COLORS AND SWIRLING CARTOON-LIKE PICTURES. GRADUALLY HE BECAME AWARE OF A DULL PAIN. AS THE PAIN GREW STRONGER, THE SURROUNDING SOUNDS BECAME CLEARER—THE HUMMING OF HOSPITAL MACHINES AND A QUIET CRYING. SAMMY KNEW HE WAS BACK.

AND THEN HE LEFT
THEM, AND THE PAIN.

FOR MY
PRECIOUS ANGEL,
ANTHONY.

A DK INK BOOK

2   4   6   8   10   9   7   5   3   1

DK Publishing, Inc., 95 Madison Avenue
New York, NY 10016
Visit us on the World Wide Web at http://www.dk.com

Manufactured in the United States of America. Printed by Barton Press, Inc.
Bound by Horowitz/Rae. Book design and hand lettering by David Kooharian.
The illustrations are pen and ink and watercolor.

Library of Congress cataloging is available upon request.
ISBN 0-7894-2466-5